I RUN

Line Mørkeby

I RUN

translated by Kim Dambæk

based on the book by Anders Legarth Schmidt

OBERON BOOKS
LONDON

WWW.OBERONBOOKS.COM

First published in 2019 by Oberon Books Ltd
521 Caledonian Road, London N7 9RH
Tel: +44 (0) 20 7607 3637 / Fax: +44 (0) 20 7607 3629
e-mail: info@oberonbooks.com
www.oberonbooks.com

A catalogue record for this book is available from the British Library.

PB ISBN: 9781786827920
E ISBN: 9781786827937

Cover photography by Fay Summerfield

Printed and bound by 4EDGE Limited, Hockley, Essex, UK.
eBook conversion by Lapiz Digital Services, India.

ABOUT CUT THE CORD

Our work focuses on new Nordic plays and promoting inter-cultural collaboration in the UK. We explore social issues through bold visual narratives and movement, questioning what it means to be human. Following our award-winning production of the Norwegian play *Kinder K* by Kristofer Grønskag, we present the UK premiere of *I Run*. Other productions include *Endless Second* by Theo Toksvig-Stewart and *Beyond the Blue* by Omnibus Young Company.

In 2020 we are curating our first Nordic Festival in London: New Nordics, in collaboration with the Nordic Ministry, Nordic Culture Fund, the Danish Arts Foundation and the Nordic embassies in the UK – celebrating contemporary Nordic theatre and presenting six new plays from Denmark, Sweden, Norway, Finland, Iceland and the Faroe Islands.

Max Keeble – Actor

Max Keeble is a British actor who trained at Drama Centre London.
Theatre credits include: *Faithful Ruslan* (Belgrade Theatre Trust and
KP Productions), *An Honourable Man* (White Bear Theatre), *Maurice*
(Above the Stag Theatre), *I Run* (Cut the Cord), *An Enemy of the
People* (Here Now Ensemble).

Screen credits include: *Strangers* (ITV).

Camilla Gürtler – Director

Camilla Gürtler is a Danish director who trained at Drama Centre
London. She is the Artistic Director of Cut the Cord and the
Emerging Creative at the h Club London 2019–20.

She also trained on StoneCrabs Theatre's Young Directors'
Programme 2013–14 and ran the Omnibus Young Company
at Omnibus Theatre 2014–19, for which she received the Jack
Petchy Leadership award. She was recently awarded a Judges'
Commendation in Directing for *Kinder K* at The National Student
Drama Festival 2018.

Directing credits include: *I Run* (Vault Festival), *Endless Second*
(Theatre503), *Beyond the Blue* (Poplar Union/Camden People's
Theatre/Theatre Royal Stratford East), *Kinder K* (National Student
Drama Festival/Bunker Theatre), *Mydidae* (Wimbledon College of
Arts), *When Mr. Excavator Came and Ate All the Trees, The Monkeys and
Hamster-Beavers Had a Battle* (Omnibus Theatre), *The Nightingale and
the Rose* (Etcetera), *An Incident at the Border* (The Albany).

Line Mørkeby – Writer

Line Mørkeby (b. 1977) is a Danish playwright. After four years of
theatre studies at the University of Copenhagen, she was admitted
at the playwriting division at Aarhus Theatre School, graduating
in 2008. The same year, her debut play *Musical* was staged at the
The Royal Theatre of Denmark with great success. In 2009 she
received the Reumert Talent-Prize for her works, and in 2010 a
Reumert for Best Play for a Young Audience for her controversial
youth drama *5EX P O C(6 P LR K)*, which was also nominated for

The Nordic Playwright Prize in 2010. That year she dazzled the audience and media with the bittersweet comedy *Joy (Lykke Bjørn)*, which secured her a nomination as Playwright of the Year and Best Play for a Small Cast. Line has received further recognition for *When It Cuts The Heart (Når Det Skærer I Hjertet)*, which was also nominated for Best Play for a Young Audience at the 2014 Reumerts; *I Me Fuck You (Jeg Mig Fuck Dig)* won the Children's Theatre Prize in 2015; and *Hair On It (Hår På Den)* was awarded the Jury Special Prize at the Reumert Awards in 2016. In 2018, she was nominated for *I Run (Jeg Løber)* – both as Playwright of the Year and for the Jury's Special Prize.

Kim Dambæk – Translator

Kim Dambæk is a translator and stage director who has worked extensively for national, regional and private theatres throughout Denmark, Norway, Sweden and Great Britain.

His translations of contemporary Nordic playwrights have been published by Oberon and Methuen and include plays by Jon Fosse, P. O. Enquist, Astrid Saalbach, Line Knutzon, Thor Bjørn Krebs, Peter Asmussen and Line Mørkeby, with productions by: Traverse Theatre, Edinburgh; BBC TV; Royal Shakespeare Company; Young Vic, London; Rough Magic Theatre, Dublin; Dogstar Theatre, Scotland; BAM Majestic Theatre, New York as well as Cut the Cord Theatre.

Niall McKeever – Designer

A recent graduate from Theatre Design at Wimbledon College of Art, Niall McKeever is an emerging London designer who has worked as a sculptor on HBO's Emmy Award Winning *Game of Thrones* for three years. In 2017 Niall worked in the Art Department on the latest Peter Strickland film *In Fabric.*

Niall's recent design work includes Seedtime's production of *Little Shop of Horrors*, directed by Susan Raasay. He is currently working on a new play, *The World We Made*, adapted by Beth Flintoff from Jonathan Porritt's book *The World We Made: Alex McKay's Story from*

2050, directed by Sophie Austin, which will premiere at Change Festival in October. Niall is currently Production Design Assistant at the National Theatre, where he is Associate Designer alongside Rae Smith on Brian Friel's *Translations* and Design Assistant on *Peter Gynt*, designed by Richard Hudson and directed by Jonathan Kent.

Sarah Carton – Composer

Sarah Carton is an award-winning musician, theatre maker and sound designer. Sarah was a Resident Artist at The Roundhouse 2018–2019 and is the Founder and Artistic Director of Rose Eye Productions: an alternative music and theatre collective, specialising in gig-theatre and spoken word. Her solo gig-theatre show *Hatch*, exploring the women's prison system, won both the Camden People's Theatre Award and Oberon Books Best New Play Award at the National Student Drama Festival 2018.

Performance credits include: *Hatch* (Rose Eye Productions: Camden People's Theatre, Etcetera Theatre, Latitude Festival, NSDF 2018), *The Theban Motherf*cker* (Action To The Word: Latitude Festival 2018).

Sound Design and Composition credits include: *Girls At Night On The Internet* (The Playground, Omnibus Theatre 2019), *Amygdala* (Chapel Playhouse 2019), *I Run* (Vaults 2019, Drama Centre 2018), *Laundry* (The Space 2018).

Charlotte Brown – Stage Manager

Since graduating from The University of Greenwich, Charlotte has plunged herself into the industry and worked her way onto what will now be her eleventh production as Stage Manager. Former credits include: *Head-Rot Holiday* (written by Sarah Daniels, directed by Will Maynard) as Assistant Director and Stage Manager, *Open* (Weighed In Productions) and *I Run* (Cut The Cord) at The Vaults Festival. She has worked with The Space on numerous productions including *Laundry*, *South Afreakins* and *The Conductor* as Lighting Designer and Operator. She joins Cut the Cord with *I Run* and *Endless Second* at The Pleasance in Edinburgh Fringe as Stage Manager.

SPECIAL THANKS TO:

h Foundation, The Embassy of Denmark, Children with Cancer, Puregym, Hummel, The Children's Cancer and Leukaemia Group, International Performance Rights Agency, Nordiska, Drama Centre London, and Ludwig Meslet.

DAY 0

Eternal weightless love till the end of time

I repeat

Eternal weightless love till the end of time

Eternal

Weightless

Love

I whisper your name

Ellen

I cry it to the heavens

Let her name colour you

Show me a rainbow over the hospital

Give me a sign she's arrived safely

That she is somewhere

That she is

Now that she's no longer here

The hospital

I have to get out of here

With the little that remains of her

A porter clicks off the brake on the hospital bed

And turns down the corridor to the lifts

The sheet

Clean

White

Crisp

The sheet

It's my last glimpse of her

I have to get out of here

The porter shoves a key into a slot making the next lift stop

He stands waiting for a while, with Ellen

It's my last glimpse of her

He rolls her into the lift

It's my last glimpse of her

He stands next to her, for a moment, before the doors shut

It's my last glimpse of her

It feels like an eternity

It's my last glimpse of her

The porter shoves a key into a small box in the lift

So it goes directly down to the basement

So it doesn't make any stops

So people visiting maternity wards

Don't accidentally meet Ellen

Under the sheet

In the lift

On the way down

To a basement below the hospital

The doors shut

That

Is my last glimpse of her

I have to get out of here

DAY 0, PLUS 1 HOUR

It's an hour since we left the hospital

Ellen's Mum, Ellen's younger sister and me

The three of us

Ellen is lying in a refrigerated room

Her belongings in a box

I

Carry that box

Ellen's Mum can't carry that box

The final drawings

A *Sleeping Beauty* DVD

Her clothes

Her clothes

It's an hour since the porter rolled her away

It's the first hour after the last hour

It's an hour after for the very last time

It's the first hour of eternity

I ought to sit down, indifferently

I ought to scream

I ought to cry

I ought to throw something and smash something

I ought to vanish with my vanished child

But I'm still here

I want to get out

Up

Who are you?

You, with my Ellen

Where are you?

I'm crying out to you

Let her name colour you

So I might see you

I will find you

You, carrying my eternal weightless love

The soul of my soul

In your arms

Out and up

Grant my legs the will

To place one foot in front of the other

Place one foot in front of the other

And the other in front of the one

One in front of the other

The other in front of the one

Again

One in front of the other

The other in front of the one

Again and again

A little faster

Until I'm running

Towards the sea. The fortress. Onto the walls.

And around

Another round

Another go

Faster

And then

Then!

I feel light

I start to soar

Not a lot

Just a little

The fortress is like a pentagonal air shaft through which I inhale

A castle

I mount it with my feet

I conquer it with my legs

I master it with my feet

Faster

And faster

My feet

Lift off the ground

Glide for an instant

Only to land once more

Repeat

Repeat, repeat, repeat

Eternally

The glide

A fraction of a second

Neither of my feet touch the ground simultaneously

I lose control of the ground

The longer I lose ground control

The longer I glide

Fractions

Become seconds

Become minutes

I count them

Add them

I land

I soar again

And every time I soar

I glide

Towards Ellen

The longer I can fly

The closer

I can come

To Ellen

Fly

Land

Fly

Land

Fly

Land

Fly

Land

Fly

Land

Fly

Land

Fly

Land

Fly

Land

Fly

Land

Flyyyyyyyyyyyyyyyyyyyyyyy

Elllllllllllllllllllllllllllllllllllllllllennnnnnnnnnnnnnnnnnnnnnnnnnn!

We are

Free!!

We are

Free!!!

Yes we can

We can

Conquer anything

Yes we can conquer anything

Aaaaannnnnyyyyytttttthhhhhiiiiinnnnnggggg

   He stops.

After six miles I get overtaken

Ellen's tiny body lies in a refrigerated room under the hospital

The earth under my feet collapses

Heaven is hell, for it has time

Heaven is hell, for it has eternity

Heaven is hell, for it has Ellen

No rainbows to show the way

A couple of trainers

Keep me fastened to the ground

A headband

Keeps my brain in place

But this is when it begins

DAY PLUS 1

The next day I do it all over again

I run

There's some magnetic gravitational pull between my
trainers and the innermost centre of the earth

Today I can't soar

It's heavy on earth

My legs have locked themselves tight

My feet are nailed down

My brain has only one choice

Ellen?

Hi Dad

How are you?

I'm fine

Are you?

Amazing

Is it beautiful?

It's SO beautiful. You can look forward to it. Try closing your eyes

But then I can't see anything

Yes you can

What can I see?

The rainbow. It shines so bright it's good your eyes are closed

Yes. I see it. Shall I follow it?

Do you really see it, or are you just pretending?

I really see it

Then follow it with your eyes

Right…

What do you see?

I see the light. Like when you danced in Pippiland

Are you afraid?

*No… Yes, I'm afraid! But I'll do it anyway, I'll do it now…
Now… And I won't ever be afraid again. Never be afraid… Oh,
Nangijala! The place beyond the stars, I see the light! I see the light!
I really do see it Ellen*

Do you?

Yes

Are you crying?

I'm howling

It's not that sad, really

Yes it is, Ellen

Ellen?

We're connected

Right Ellen?

Our souls are connected

Right Ellen?

Our souls are connected by these gravel paths

Right now

These gravel paths are threads connecting me to you

Right Ellen?

Ellen?

DAY PLUS 2

Ellen's Mum?

Ellen's Mum

I unlock the door to the flat

Ellen's Mum sits on the windowsill in the living room

She's holding onto the box with Ellen's things

She stares at Ellen's drawing

The one of the balloon

Doesn't look up

When I enter

Is so immobile

Ellen's heart

Lay in Ellen's Mum's body

My breathing fills the room

With the sound of life

But I can't breathe for her as well

So I sidestep

Away from the walls

Leave her

Wide open

Shut the door behind me

Down onto the street

Switch on my watch

And the next day becomes two days later becomes three days later becomes four days later becomes

DAY PLUS 5

Flowers

A bouquet

I sidestep

A gravel path

A newly pruned hedge

More flowers

A whitewashed wall

A face

I sidestep

Another bouquet

A face

A granddad

A hymn book

A pastor

I sidestep

A church pew

An altar

I sidestep

A coffin

A coffin

A coffin

Locks me to the ground I can't soar

A gravestone

My legs

Are nailed to the ground

I tug at them

To get them free

But fall

I rise

Tug

Fall

Rise

Tug

Fall

Rise

Tug hard

Tug my feet free

Of nails

Shred my feet

Open

The glide

The speed

The breath

The soar

The speed

The breath

Its own small rhythm

Its own symphony

Its own creation

It

Never ends

Ellen

In the coffin

Driven away

That

Is my last glimpse of her

Ellen in the coffin

The coffin

The coffin

Is my last

Glimpse

Of her

DAY MINUS 801

Ellen dances

Bum dance

Ellen's younger sister lies on a rug

Ellen dances

Naked

Round about the flat

She's just had a bath

Her hair's newly combed

Her cheeks are flushed

She dances

Careless

Free

Bum dance

Dum dum gong dum dum gong

Bum dance

Dances

Sings

Dum dum gong dum dum gong

Wiggles her little bum

Careless

Carelessly free

We just observe

Ellen's Mum and I

Dum dum gong dum dum gong

DAY PLUS 6

The day after the funeral, I meet the Poet

The Poet runs up alongside me

The Poet runs in FiveFingers

His long hair hanging loose

Shades, so I can't see where he's looking

In a neon green sweat suit

Pink headband

He's strong though he doesn't look strong

We're the same age

We don't know anything about each other

Both just run

He lays a hand on me and says

Just want you to know that

I of course know what's happened to your daughter

*What you and her Mum and her younger sister are going through
Just want you to know that…*

I can't begin to imagine your pain

But I feel for you

And if I could carry some of your pain, I would

We run together for a while

Gong gong

Gong gong

Dum dum

Dum dum gong

Dum dum gong gong

Dum dum gong dum dum gong gong dum dum gong dum
dum gong gong dum dum gong dum dum gong gong dum
dum gong dum dum gong gong dum dum gong dum dum
gong gong

I get what he sees

He sees

Me running fast

He sees

Me bearing it on my own

He sees

Himself lagging behind

He sees

There's a way

I haven't seen myself

He sees that

I sense it

DAY PLUS 11

The graveyard

Ellen's gravestone

She felt life bubbling inside her

Is written on the gravestone

Try to lift it

And run off with it

Give up

Place it down

Start again

Lift it

Place it

Start again

Lift it

Up

Run with it through town

Past the park

The hospital

The ponds

Past all the dark

And to where

I am no longer bound to the ground

Now the gravestone becomes light

I can carry it

It lifts off the ground and glides with me

The skull splits

The headband snaps

The head opens up

The brain pours out

And everything lifts itself out of me

It

Soars

Words

Thoughts

Sorrow

Longing

All the dark

It

Pours out of me

Past my body

Past my head

I never again want to stand on my legs I never again want to understand my legs they shall remain under me always always be lowest even when I fall always the heart above the feet always the brain above the heart always the feet rushing through me I realize I know I can I dance Ellen happy Ellen dances happily happy child can we yes we can and we shall meet one day if I just keep this way open I can soar I can glide don't stop me Ellen's Mum I love you but don't stop me it's pouring it's shining it's just words now words thoughts dark verses streaming stop for a minute there I lost myself for a minute not in a million cry me a river I just wanna I just gotta I got too much life running through my veins going to waste the sky is not the limit that is why I keep on running can you keep up can all of you keep up fuckers I can I can I can hand me a nail and I'll swallow it raw I step on it I run with it in my foot if need be be as it may 'cause there are no fucking tears in heaven and somewhere over the rainbow we are the heroes there is no one to help us or save us you dance Ellen we feel life bubbling inside us don't we Ellen we are heroes Ellen we are heroes we can be heroes and I

He sings 'Heroes' by David Bowie.

DAY PLUS 17

Distance

17

Pulse

187

Time

1:39

17 miles

Max pulse 187

In 1 hour and 39 minutes

99 minutes

My 99 minutes

I didn't know I could

I didn't know I could own time

I didn't know I could move in time

So fast

DAY MINUS 708

A forest lake

We've rented a house in Sweden

I catch a pike

Ellen looks at it with her big round eyes

And it looks at her

We slice it in pieces and fry it in a pan

We pick blueberries place them in dough and bake
cinnamon swirls

And meet a viper

I scream and cling to Ellen

Ellen just looks at it with curiosity

It's the last summer before the illness

Our last summer in ignorance

DAY PLUS 25

I can't stand looking at the photos of Ellen

I can't stand looking at the photos of Ellen

I can't stand looking at the photos of Ellen

I can't stand looking at the photos of Ellen

I can't stand looking at the photos of Ellen

I can't stand looking at the photos of Ellen

I can't live with the memories

I can't live without them

DAY PLUS 26

I try to work

DAY PLUS 27

I try building Lego with Ellen's younger sister

DAY PLUS 28

The photos appear on my computer

Ellen by the forest lake

I crawl into bed

Day becomes night

DAY PLUS 29

Night becomes day

Run

Eat

Work

DAY PLUS 30

Becomes night

DAY PLUS 32

Dark

DAY PLUS 39

Run

DAY PLUS 44

Becomes night

DAY PLUS 51

Becomes day

Work through it

Becomes night

DAY PLUS 60

Dark

DAY PLUS 67

Run

Sleep

DAY PLUS 68

Running

Sleeping

DAY PLUS 69

Sleeping while I run

DAY PLUS 71

Running while I sleep

DAY PLUS 72

She's gone

She won't be back

I

Have to get out

I

Only feel grief

I

Will become grief

I only feel Ellen

Ellen and grief

Ellen is grief

Ellen is in me

I am grief

DAY PLUS 74

Eat

Fall asleep at 10

Wake up at midnight

Wake up at 2

Is it morning?

When the fuck is it morning?

Wake up at 4

Get up

Walk about the flat

Fall asleep again

Wake up at 6

Get up

Oatmeal with milk and sugar

And off

3 miles at an easy pace

I only eat because I have to

The pleasure of eating no longer exists

After 7 miles I'm grateful for having put sugar on the oatmeal

11 miles

As all parents, who have held their dead child in their arms, know, there is no longer any pleasure or happiness

After 13 miles the sugar's been well and truly burnt I start on the rations

Although I'm a privileged person

15.7

with access to pleasure and happiness

17.8

the privilege

18

of enjoying happiness

18.5

is no longer for me

after 20 miles the channels are open

I run into everything I don't understand

The music helps me along

The music is Ellen

Ellen is the music

I can rewind time

The faster I run

No matter how heavily I start

I end lightly

I dance

I dance into something larger

Where pleasure exists

Where happiness exists

Where I stand in front of Ellen

Where I smell her smell

Lie tucked close to her while she sleeps

It's in my body

It's all I have

That's all there is

There is no collective consciousness

There's only my own larger place

That I do know

I know everything here

Alright?

I know everything here, for Christ's sake!! Alright!!?

DAY PLUS 80

Dear God may I offer my condolences on your loss
of a human

DAY PLUS 82

19 miles

Where the fuck is it?

20 miles

The sense of freedom?

The euphoria?

Where the fuck is it?

21 miles

Where the fuck is it?

I'm not dancing today

DAY MINUS 698

Ellen dances

She thinks we're on our way home from our trip
to Sweden

We pretend to take the wrong turning

Honestly – weren't we meant to turn here?

Yes – isn't Denmark that way?

No Denmark's that way

And what's this then?

Ellen looks up and out of the car window

Pippi!!?

We must have taken a wrong turning!

Madicken!!?

Ronja!!?

Lionheart!!?

Nangijala

Gosh – we've landed in Pippi Longstocking Land, Ellen

How on earth did that happen?

I suppose we'd better stay here for a couple of days then

Ellen dances with delight

She's standing by the entrance

There's music from an orchestra

And she's wiggling her tiny bum

The only one dancing

But she carries on

Up on her toes

Down again

Holding onto her sun hat

Closes her eyes

I want it to continue

I'm happy

It mustn't stop

She feels life bubbling inside her

It mustn't stop

It's her paradise on earth

Everyone smiles at her

The world smiles at her

It's her land

It's her world

And right on the other side

The after life

Nangijala

DAY PLUS 83

The memory catches up with me and I increase speed

Need to run

My pulse needs to find a satellite

Need to run fast now

Otherwise that little nasty, evil, evil word will catch up
with me

Memory

I lose my breath

Breathless

I can hardly catch my breath

184 pulse beats per minute

The blood is pumping through my body

185

Faster than my vessels can keep up

My heart screams

Stop

186

The base of my lungs are being torn to shreds

They beg

187

Plead me to stop

For peace

188

I can't catch my breath

But that's when

That's when I have to continue

Right then, when everything else disappears

And vanishes

189

DAY MINUS 616

Ellen

Ellen look

Bricks

Shall we build a tower?

Sorry

How long do we have to wait?

We've been here for almost an hour now

The secretary looks up:

Uhm, I think he

He's just making a call

Calling who?

Just a moment

Can you please tell me what's going on

It's only a blood test

He said we'd get the results straight away

She's only got a sore throat

The secretary goes into the doctor's office

The waiting room is full

Ellen

That's a fine tower you've built

The secretary

You can see him now

Ellen

Ellen

Come

Yes come on

We can take the bricks with us

Come on let's take the bricks along

The doctor

Come in

Fine bricks you've brought along

Ellen

The doctor

The temporary doctor

Our GP is on holiday

The temporary doctor:

Right... I just had to make a call

Right? To whom?

Temporary doctor

Sweaty hands

To your GP

He's on holiday

Right...

Ellen

Look Dad

Uh oh it's falling

Aahh

Watch out Dad

It's falling

The temporary doctor

Right, well I just wanted to go through some things with your own doctor

Right? But he's on holiday!?

Yes...he is, but...

What was it you wanted to go through with our GP?

Thing is I don't know Ellen as a patient so

Ellen

Look Dad

Let me just get this clear

Right, it's because Ellen's blood count

Yes, what about it?

Ellen

Look Dad

Yes my love

Right, well it's...it is...uncommonly low

Ellen

Look Dad

It's falling

It may not mean anything

No? Right? What then?

Temporary doctor

Book an appointment with your GP. As soon as he's back from holiday. And have some extensive tests done

It's falling

Ellen

Look Dad

The tower is falling

Ellen

Is falling

Little Ellen

Inside little Ellen's body

Sick cells are making

Healthy cells fall apart

DAY PLUS 94

This is my advice to me:

Stay healthy

Don't fall

Stay healthy

Don't fall

Stay healthy

Don't fall

Stay healthy

Stay healthy

Don't fall

Stay healthy

Don't fall

Stay healthy

Don't fall

Don't fall

I'm falling

Getting up

Fall

Get up

Run

Fall

Run

Fall

Get up

Fall

Get up

Fall

Get up

Fall

Get up

Fall

Run

DAY PLUS 98

Half marathon

Run 13 miles

In 1 hour and 15 minutes

I can do it

Start number 980

Pink headband

1 hour and 15 minutes

75 minutes

75

That's the number

That's my number

That's my limit

I hope I can

Within the limit

I don't know if I can

But I hope

Hope

Hope has a limit

Eternity kills you

That's why I want to

That's why I want to be able to

That's why there's a limit

'Cause outside that limit

Everything falls apart

75

That's my limit

Come on

1 mile

Doubt is a vulture

Circling over my head

Trying to land on my shoulder

3 miles

I lash out at the vulture

Manage to keep it at a distance

5 miles

But then

New street

7 miles

I imagine the finish line

They'll be there

Hopeful

Ellen's Mum

Ellen's younger sister

But not Ellen

Then it dives

Then it lands on my shoulder

Then it sinks its claws

Into my flesh

Strikes its beak against my skull

The sound

Of nails scratching on a blackboard

I feel no pain

But I feel the weight

Muscles

Lungs

Breath

Are out of play

Only my head now

Grim thoughts

Against weary legs

Dark thoughts

Nourishing the vulture

Picking them like meaty lumps

Straight out of my brain

Freedom

The glide

Willpower

Hacking them to shreds with its beak

But then I see him

The Poet

Neon green jacket

The Poet isn't running

He's gliding

50 metres ahead

My salvation

I think

If I can make it up alongside the Poet

I'll be able to knock the vulture down

I'll be able to bash it away

Poet!

Wait for me Poet!

Slow down Poet!

I'm now 10 metres away from him

The vulture flaps its wings

Feathers glide down onto the ground in front of me

With every step I take

I kick them away Poet!

Wait for me

The Poet's neon green back grows smaller and smaller

He finally disappears completely

What's happening?

He was right in front of me

I was almost there

Has he increased speed?

No

I've decreased speed

Weighed down by the vulture on my shoulder

It's just the two of us now

The vulture and I

Neither of us fly

Breathing is painful

The lungs tighten

The air can't get down deep enough

Can't make its way to the lung tissue

Can't transport the oxygen around my body

That's how Ellen felt before she died

Her lungs were full of tiny scratches

The oxygen couldn't pass through

The pain

Ellen's pain is in me

A roar erupts

Right before the finish line

I flap my arms

Like they were wings

Like they could make me soar

The vulture lets go of its hold

Ellen's Mum

Ellen's younger sister

They cheer

Hopeful

The finish line

75 minutes 52 seconds

Doubt devoured 52 seconds

Further away a vulture sits on the ground

Gobbling up dark thoughts like lumps of prey

DAY MINUS 567

We've received the results from Ellen's blood test
Yes?
Our GP is back from holiday

It still looks wonky

Wonky? What's that?

Ellen's got to have extensive tests done, right now, at the hospital. It's urgent.

Urgent

What kind of small unpleasant word is that

How can six letters, by themselves so fine, become such an unpleasant expression

when put together like that?

The conversation room

How can two words like conversation and room,
by themselves so fine, become such

an unpleasant phrase when strung together?

Ellen's blue patches won't go away

More and more appear

On top of each other

We go to the hospital

More tests

The blood count is still low

Can't explain the blue patches

Extensive tests

Urgent

Extensive tests

We wait

Filter coffee

No appetite

Foul hours

And then

The conversation room

Ellen has leukaemia

Ellen has what?

Leukaemia

What?

Cancer of the blood

I bloody well know what leukaemia is

Foul words

Foul foul words

DAY PLUS 107

Grief support group

One life-shattering account after another

Ellen's Mum

Sits uneasy

Still she sits

More than can be said for me

Andreas and Penelope

Lost little Carl

The last day of spring

Andreas recounts

Penelope cries

Penelope recounts

Andreas cries

The tray with strawberries and nuts

Does the rounds

Travelling among grief stricken hands

Trying to comfort

Those beyond the grasp of comfort

I get up

And run off

I wanted to say

I'm the father of a dead daughter

It's the ultimate loss of control

Ellen's body withered

And died

A run is exactly the opposite

It is

The ultimate form of control

I can steer the body down to its finest detail

Down to a second

I decide

The cancer cells decide nothing

I can't sit here eating strawberries

And nuts

With you

I decide

I love

I sleep

I eat

I write

I cry

I kiss

I decide

I speak

I blink

I shake

I crawl

I fall

I miss

I scream

I run

I forget

DAY PLUS 108

It's not a flight

It's a hunt

It's not a flight

It's a hunt

It's not a flight

It's a hunt

It's not a flight

It's a hunt

It's not a flight

It's a hunt

DAY MINUS 428

A small wheelchair

An oxygen apparatus

Ellen can't catch her breath

The hospital

Panic

What's going on?

It'll be alright

She's stable again

You can go home now

More panic

Ambulance

Oxygen flasks

Respirator

Tubes

Doctors

More doctors

White coats

What's going on? Would someone please tell me?

Just a minute

Face mask

Bacteria

Careful

If you could just move slightly

If you would just stand over there

Injection

Anaesthetic

Induced coma

Tube feeding

Out of induced coma

She is stable

But then

She can't breathe

More panic

What's going on?

Oxygen apparatus

It's under control

Everything's fine

For now

DAY MINUS 398

Ellen's lungs start getting more and more damaged

A complication in relation to the cancer treatment

She's getting ill through the attempts to cure her

Her lungs become hard

Can't pump properly

But Ellen will manage

God knows

She will manage

It's not out of my hands

IT'S NOT OUT OF MY HANDS

RIGHT!?

D'YOU HEAR ME?

DO YOU WANT PROOF THAT I BELIEVE?

IS THAT IT?

DO YOU WANT TO SEE ME PRAY?

IS THAT IT?

DO YOU WANT TO SEE ME GET DOWN, WEEPING,
ON MY KNEES, FOLD MY HANDS AND

CRY TO THE HEAVENS?

Is that it?

'Cause I'll happily do so

I will

Believe me, I will

DAY PLUS 134

Darkness

Completely dark

I'm completely dark today

And I run straight into everything dark

And look for a way out

And right then

Right then

When the darkness is about to devour me

Conquer me

Demolish me

That's when I meet the Poet

Well, if it isn't the Man With the Headband

May I run along with you?

DAY PLUS 143

I'm the man with the headband. I run on God, the Father
Almighty, creator of heaven and earth.

I run on fucking Jesus Christ, God's only Son, Our Lord.
I run on the Holy Spirit, the holy, common church, the
Holy Communion, the forgiveness of sins, the resurrection
of the body and the life everlasting. Amen

DAY PLUS 187

I've got a stone in my shoe

I've got a stone in my shoe

I've got a stone in my shoe

I've got a stone in my shoe

I've got a stone in my shoe

I've got a stone in my shoe

I've got a stone in my shoe

I've got a stone in my shoe

I've got a stone in my shoe

I've got a stone in my shoe

I've got a stone in my shoe

I've got a stone in my shoe

I've got a stone in my shoe

I've got a stone in my shoe

I've got a stone in my shoe

I've got a stone in my shoe

I've got a stone in my shoe

I've got a stone in my shoe

I've got a stone in my shoe

I've got a stone in my shoe

I've got a stone in my shoe

I've got a stone in my shoe

I've got a stone in my shoe

I've got a stone in my shoe

I've got a nail in my foot

I've got nails in my feet

I've got knives in my feet

I've got feet that are shredded to bits

I've got blood coming out of my toes

I've got blood

DAY MINUS 366

It's fine to go for a walk

Ellen is stable

So you're okay to go for a walk

The nurse smiles

Ellen's favourite

You and your Dad

You can go for a walk

Do you want to go for a walk, Ellen?

Ellen nods

The National Gallery?

Ellen nods

She has trouble catching her breath

So she nods

And whispers

Come on Dad!

She's in her wheelchair

She whispers

The respirator means she can only whisper

Are you coming Dad, or shall I go on my own?

Shall we take the path through the cemetery?

She nods

Tiny little person with her tiny little head

It's summer

We turn into the cemetery

Ellen looks at the stones

She lifts her hand as a signal for me to stop

Points at a gravestone with a palette and brush
engraved on it

Fine artist

She whispers

Fine artist

Oh such delicate small words

She almost can't catch enough breath to say them

Catch breath

Catch her breath

Is it something you catch?

Is it something you fucking well have to catch?

DAY PLUS 190

'Tears in Heaven' by Eric Clapton plays.

Oh shut up

'Tears in Heaven' by Eric Clapton plays.

Shut the fuck up

'Tears in Heaven' by Eric Clapton plays.

Oh please

'Tears in Heaven' by Eric Clapton plays.

Would you please shut up

'Tears in Heaven' by Eric Clapton plays.

Shut up there are no tears in heaven

Stay healthy

Don't fall

Stay healthy

Don't fall

Stay healthy

Don't fall

Stay healthy

Don't fall

Stay healthy

Don't fall

Stay healthy

Don't fall

Stay healthy

Don't fall

Stay healthy

Don't fall

Stay healthy

Don't fall

DAY PLUS 245

Visit Ellen's grave

Can't just stand here

Honouring her memory

So I sink

I sink down

Become one with the ground

I sink

Sinking into the earth

Dissolving

Can't just stand here

No one's coming to save me

No one's coming to save me

No one's coming to save me

No one's coming to save me

No one's coming to save me

No one's coming to save me

I'm chanting to myself

No one's coming to save me

There is no salvation

No reconciliation

No one to carry me

DAY PLUS 246

246 days after Ellen dies

Ellen's Mum gives Ellen's younger sister a bath

I try joining them

I try to get my legs to obey and join them

To sit on the edge of the tub and have a moment
with them

A completely normal, everyday moment between
a Mum, a Dad, a daughter and a bathtub

But my legs move elsewhere

They don't want to

They don't want to join in

Or they can't

They won't

They can't

They won't

They can't

Fall

Onto the floor

Up the wall

Into the wall

Off the ceiling

The wall's the floor

The floor's the wall

The ceiling's the floor

The wall's the ceiling

My head lands

Into the wall

Onto the floor

Down on the ceiling

First they appear as small stabs from the diaphragm

Convulsions

Like vomit

It rises through my throat

Pressing itself through my mouth

Animal noises that aren't mine

Vomit them up and all over myself

Moan

Moan

Moan

Slide down the wall

And land on the ceiling

The floor above me

Melt onto my weeping knees

My weeping knees for Christ's sake

Hammer fists onto floor, forehead, wall, doorframe, ceiling, chest, head, floor, forehead, wall, doorframe, ceiling, chest, head, floor, forehead, wall, doorframe, ceiling, chest, head, ceiling, head, ceiling, head oh you fucking head

My head in Ellen's Mum's hands

Pull yourself together

Pull yourself together for Christ's sake, man

Ellen's younger sister is sitting right in there in the bath, for God's sake

She can bloody well hear you

She can bloody well hear your moaning

How do you think that makes her feel?

I move out the next day

The loss is complete

The pain has outshone itself

DAY MINUS 219

The hospital

Blood transfusion

Transplantation of stem cells

Might possibly save Ellen's life

Fifty Fifty

What's that?

50 50

Two numbers

My child's chances of survival

Will be one

Or the other

And although both numbers are equal

One number is beauty, life, happiness

And the other number is darkness, death, grief

A smile from a nurse on the ward

The smile of pain

As if she's smiling to keep our spirits high

Though it looks bleak

Though it looks like a fifty fifty chance

Fifty fifty

She'll make it

She won't make it

She'll make it

She won't make it

She'll make it

She won't make it

Believe in good

Lose to evil

Believe in good

Lose to evil

Believe in good

Lose to evil

Believe in good

Lose to evil

Fifty fifty

DAY PLUS 319

Ellen sits on my back now

Light as a feather

She lifts me off the ground

Keeps me soaring full of all my love for her

It flows all the way from every single cell of my
living body

It flows from me into her

Making us both weightless

She is with me

DAY MINUS 134

The dress

The one with the vertical stripes

Ellen sits with her back to me on the hospital bed

She draws

A drawing of a little girl floating with a balloon in
her hand

Across the rooftops

A little masterpiece

Of beauty divine

Impossible to understand it's been drawn by a girl of six

The dress unfurls like a cape beneath her

As if she's flying away

As if she'll soon glide away

DAY PLUS 365

Stormy

Early morning

Waiting for the Poet

Where the fuck is he?

He should have been here ages ago

It's 6:35

The wind chill factor is minus 2000

When he finally appears

He's moving at a snail's pace like it's bloody Via Dolorosa

*You say you'd like to carry some of my burden for me if you could
why the fuck do you say so when you can't and why the fuck
don't you if you can perhaps because you don't mean it well stop
saying such bullshit then if you don't mean it yes I'm pissed off this
morning I'm pissed off 'cause you come meandering along some
2000 years late and furthermore take no fucking responsibility for
all the things you say you will take responsibility for yes what the
fuck did you expect my daughter's dead I can't run back and find
her I'm bloody well aware of that I can only run forwards and find
her within myself is that what you mean is it are you telling me I
can't run from the grief over my daughter's death I can only run
with the grief over my daughter's death are you telling me that I
have no need of your advice I need you to be bloody responsible for
arriving too late and for you to swallow your own empty promises
everything is dark completely dark there's no heaven no eternity*

Ellen's gone dark dead demolished does not exist no one helps
mankind and I've overtaken you on the inside and the outside and
above and below a long time ago 'cause you're not someone I can
bloody rely on and today is the anniversary it's day plus 365 365
days since the final hour and nothing helps, there is nothing

DAY PLUS 366

Becomes one year and a day since the final hour becomes
one year and two days since the final hour becomes one
year and three days since the final hour becomes

DAY PLUS 370

When needing becomes loving when loving becomes
wear me down then skin me raw when raw becomes
exposure when exposure becomes that shame when
that shame becomes my heart, it bleeds, when that heart
becomes that muscle that keeps needing more and more
and when needing becomes loving and loving becomes
wear me down then skin me raw when raw becomes
exposure when exposure becomes that shame when
that shame becomes my heart, it reeks, when that heart
becomes that muscle that keeps needing more and more
and when needing becomes loving and loving becomes
wear me down then skin me raw my thoughts disappear if
I command strength like I command my legs , 'cause it's
just, it's just, it's just the heart that becomes that muscle
that just needs more and more that just needs more and
more for me to carry on otherwise Ellen will disappear

DAY PLUS 456

The graveyard

A magpie flaps in front of me

A beetle tickles my arm

Flies flock about my face

It's April

Perhaps the end of April

The sun is shining

And it's snowing

Tiny white flowers from the plum trees

Sprinkling down

A tiny snowflake enters my mouth

And I feel a jab somewhere in my heart

A calm

I can't remember the last time I felt it

DAY MINUS 102

The conversation with the consultant

On the wall

Two screens with pictures of Ellen's lungs

One is six months old

The other is from right now

Now

The consultant:

You see…

Ellen's illness…it's progressing. It's worsened. It won't get any
better. There's no more we can do now

Now

All hope is gone

Now

The miracle won't come

Now

The tide won't turn

Now

All is turned off

Now

It's a matter of time

Now

We are silent

Now we walk with heavy steps over to our darling lying
in the hospital bed

Now

She looks up at us with big round green eyes and smiles

Now

DAY PLUS 478

The craving for speed

When the body needs more oxygen than I can supply

Ellen

Her body needed more oxygen than she could supply

I hit 13 miles an hour

Lose all control

Head is empty

Nothing inside

It has to stop right now

This suffering has to stop now

Take me away

Save me

It's out of my hands

But it's not out of my legs

DAY PLUS 483

Run through the graveyard

A magpie flaps and soars into my head

A sore in my leg starts playing up

Do another round

Repeat

A magpie flaps and soars into my head

A sore in my leg gets worse

A beetle

Up my nose a fly in my eye a spider in my mouth

Do another round

Repeat

A magpie flaps and soars into my head

A sore in my leg gets worse and worse

Do another round

Repeat

A sore in my leg won't disappear

I open my mouth and scream without sound

I do another round

I repeat

Sore

I do another round

I repeat

Sore

I am sore

I open my mouth and scream without sound

A snowstorm of white flower flakes from the plum tree
gush forth

DAY PLUS 543

Sore

Ill from running

And I have a marathon to run in 2 months

Fever and pain in the lungs

It's as if my body is saying stop

But I want to go out again

I don't want to stop

Don't want red lights

I don't want quiet sofa small cup of tea with honey and a magazine full of trivialities

I run!

That's what I am!

DAY PLUS 550

I run again

My doctor says I shouldn't run the marathon

My physio says fifty fifty chance of getting me ready in time

Up

Out

Off

Run

Sleep

Run

Sleep

The road

The bed

Life

Death

Soar

Land

I must run the marathon in 2:41

I must live with the longing for Ellen every day

I must live with the dark

I won't live an ordinary life

Where people discuss trivialities

And banalities

Ordinariness

Gosh where did you get those steaks

And what school will your daughter attend

None of the ordinary makes any sense to me

I won't live that life

I shall live a life with a close relationship to my dead daughter

Ellen

And to Ellen's younger sister

Alice

Alice

DAY PLUS 551

Alice

The living daughter

She kissed her dead older sister and couldn't understand why she didn't

Kiss her back

DAY PLUS 552

Alice

The living daughter

I lie close to her while she's asleep and hold her tight

Smell her smell

She lives in the shadow of her dead sister

Alice

I want a close relationship with you

And your mum

Freja

DAY PLUS 554

Freja

Freja

Freja?

I want to be close to you and Alice

DAY PLUS 610

There's a strawberry growing on Ellen's grave

Coming out of her earth

I eat the strawberry

It tastes heavenly

DAY MINUS 13

Ellen's best friend comes to visit at the hospital

Ellen's friend

Ellen, I've heard you're going to die

What the fuck have those parents told their kid

Here we are trying to avoid Ellen finding out

Here we are trying to protect Ellen

Ellen doesn't reply

She doesn't have enough air to reply

At first

But then she replies:

Oh noo. You're so silly

Of course I'm not going to die

Ellen smiles

The girlfriend polishes Ellen's nails

They watch *The Little House on the Prairie*

While holding hands

DAY PLUS 624

Alice

The living daughter

I'll erace you Dad

Erace you

Okay let's

We erace all the way to the gate

We're off to Morocco

Alice

Freja

And me

Alice learns to swim

On a beach

In Morocco

She learns to swim

Without water wings

While Ellen swims with her wings somewhere else

Now

They're both swimming

In their own place

Now

Now is for the child

Now is for Alice

Now is for Ellen

This now is for you Ellen

We dance

Alice dances for joy

She can swim

She dances with Ellen's Mum

She dances with Freja

On a beach

And we write Ellen's name in the sand

And the heavens open

Merging her name with the sand

Merging time with this now

Ellen emerges

She is in this now

And in this

With Alice

Freja

And me

And a rainbow high in the sky

My little life artist

My little fine artist

The sky takes colour from your name

DAY MINUS 5

Ellen twists in the hospital bed

I can't breathe – turn it up

DAY PLUS 745

5 days till the marathon

I'm ready

2:41

Yes I can

DAY MINUS 4

Ellen twists in the hospital bed

I can't breathe – turn it up

DAY PLUS 746

4 days till the marathon

I'm ready

2:41

Yes I can

DAY MINUS 3

Ellen twists in the hospital bed

I can't breathe – turn it up

I can't breathe – turn it up

DAY PLUS 749

The pain Ellen suffered during her short time on earth can't be compared to anything else

A marathon is a parody of suffering

I'm a machine

I love the sensation of overtaking others

I'm on my own

DAY MINUS 1

The last night

I sleep in another room though you are dying

I look at the watch and wish time would vanish though this is my last time on earth with you

I can't handle you

Ellen

Why don't I lie in your bed on your last night when I know you are dying

Sorry Ellen

Sorry

DAY PLUS 750

Marathon

I'm a runner

I'm a front runner

I'm Ellen's Dad

Ellen's life was my responsibility

I can never let go of the guilt

I can't breathe – turn it up

She floats away

I sink

I pull myself up again

And again

I can't breathe – turn it up

I sink

I pull myself up again

When the finish line appears

It'll say

2 hours and 41 minutes

A strawberry

I won't just wait for death

And be swallowed up by trivialities

Don't let the wind win

Those who whisper tell the truth

She felt life bubbling inside her

Alice is healthy

All the life you waste to feel alive

Alice is healthy

Alice is healthy

Alice is healthy

Alice is healthy

Alice is healthy

Alice is healthy

DAY 0

I can't breathe – turn it up

The drawing with the balloon

The girl hanging over the rooftops

She's floating away

Ellen knew she was dying

She whispers

Let me go

The road whispers

You are free

She twists

The tiny body in the huge hospital bed

Catch your breath – is it something you catch

I can't breathe – turn it up

She whispers

We make the decision

Turn it off now

She mustn't suffer any longer

I can't breathe – turn it up

She whispers

No one on earth can comprehend the depth of suffering
Ellen has endured

She mustn't suffer any longer

I can't breathe – turn it up

Then the guilt

Why didn't I sleep with her that last night

Could I have done more

Could I have put up more of a fight

Could I

Could I

Only I

Understand the depth of guilt

Only I

Only I could

Not protect my child

I pull myself up again

When the finish line appears

It'll say

2 hours and 40 minutes

I'm at the front of the race

There's a doctor

And a nurse

Freja

And me

Hour minus 24

Morphine

Ellen is no longer conscious

She's asleep

More morphine

Hour minus 20

They come and check up on us

She smiles

Ellen's favourite

And a doctor

Hour minus 13

Exhausted

Hour minus 12

I leave the ward

Can't take any more

I have to get away

Hour minus 8

Morning

I knew it was her last night

Why didn't I stay with her

Why didn't I lie with her and hold her?

I pull myself up again

When the finish line appears

It'll say

2 hours and 39 minutes

I'm at the front of the race

Hour minus 6

Ellen's chest is completely swollen

Hour minus 3 more morphine

Now the doctor and the nurse are there more and
more often

Hour minus 2

We just sit next to her

Hold her

Hour minus 1

This is it

We are ready

We would like you to turn it off now

Alright

Is she smiling?

Ellen?

Is she smiling?

No

She's suffering

Beautiful

Eternal

Weightless

Love

You're suffering

And we can do nothing

Other than let you go

You won't suffer any longer

They turn the respirator down slightly

Then slightly more

Then slightly more

Then they turn it off completely

We hold her

We are calm

And then she dies

She is beautiful

She is so beautiful

Right then

When her tiny heart stops

Zero hour

Ellen's chest falls into place

Finally

Finally

Finally

Her body is calm

Weightless

Freja sits holding her in her arms

She is the most beautiful tiny being as she lies there
in her mother's

Arms and is no longer

She no longer cries for oxygen

Her stomach is not swollen

Her face is smooth

The most beautiful tiny being

A corpse

Zero hour

I will never feel calm again

The finish line

Time

In front

Pull myself up

The finish line

2 hours and 38 minutes

The seconds

Run

The sky

Run faster

Ellen

Faster

Two hours and

Eternity

The sky

The finish line

Ellen

Ellen

The sky

The finish line

Ellen

Where are you?

Ellen

Ellen

Weightless

Run

Soar

Run

Soar

EEEEELLLLLLENN!!!

I sink

I sink

I sink

Ellen

You are in my longing

I sink

> *He runs at high speed.*
>
> *Ellen is somewhere in the room.*
>
> *He decreases speed.*
>
> *He starts walking.*
>
> *THE END.*

.